Dear Parents:

Congratulations! Your child is taking the first steps on an exciting journey. The destination? Independent reading!

STEP INTO READING® will help your child get there. The program offers five steps to reading success. Each step includes fun stories and colorful art or photographs. In addition to original fiction and books with favorite characters, there are Step into Reading Non-Fiction Readers, Phonics Readers and Boxed Sets, Sticker Readers, and Comic Readers—a complete literacy program with something to interest every child.

Learning to Read, Step by Step!

Ready to Read   Preschool–Kindergarten
• big type and easy words • rhyme and rhythm • picture clues
For children who know the alphabet and are eager to begin reading.

Reading with Help   Preschool–Grade 1
• basic vocabulary • short sentences • simple stories
For children who recognize familiar words and sound out new words with help.

Reading on Your Own   Grades 1–3
• engaging characters • easy-to-follow plots • popular topics
For children who are ready to read on their own.

Reading Paragraphs   Grades 2–3
• challenging vocabulary • short paragraphs • exciting stories
For newly independent readers who read simple sentences with confidence.

Ready for Chapters   Grades 2–4
• chapters • longer paragraphs • full-color art
For children who want to take the plunge into chapter books but still like colorful pictures.

STEP INTO READING® is designed to give every child a successful reading experience. The grade levels are only guides; children will progress through the steps at their own speed, developing confidence in their reading. The F&P Text Level on the back cover serves as another tool to help you choose the right book for your child.

Remember, a lifetime love of reading starts with a single step!

Visit us on the Web!
StepIntoReading.com
rhcbooks.com

Educators and librarians, for a variety of teaching tools, visit us at RHTeachersLibrarians.com

Library of Congress Cataloging-in-Publication Data is available upon request.
ISBN 978-0-593-56478-3 (trade) — ISBN 978-0-593-56479-0 (lib. bdg.) —
ISBN 978-0-593-56480-6 (ebook)

Printed in the United States of America
10 9 8 7 6 5 4 3

This book has been officially leveled by using the F&P Text Level Gradient™ Leveling System.

UNI'S
Uni the UNICORN
Wish for Wings

an Amy Krouse Rosenthal book
pictures based on art by Brigette Barrager

Random House 🏠 New York

Uni is watching
the birds fly.

They soar
across the sky.
It looks like fun!
Uni longs for wings.

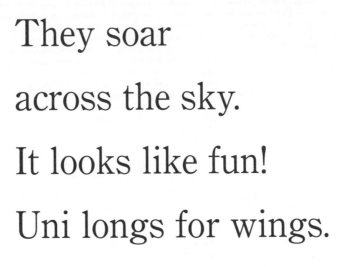

A bird sits alone
on a branch
above Uni.
It is afraid
to fly.

"You have wings,"
Uni tells the bird.
"Just flap them!"

Then Uni sees
a strange sight.
A horse with wings!

The flying horse
lands in a field.
Uni trots over.

"Hi, I am Uni."
"My name is
Pegasus,"
says the horse.
"Call me Peg."

"Why do you have wings?" Uni asks. "I was born with them," Peg says.

"I wish I could
fly," Uni says.
"I could teach you,"
says Peg.
"But you need wings."

Uni has a
magic horn.
But it will not help
Uni grow wings.

"I will make wings!"
Uni says.

Uni finds two
feathers.
Not enough
for wings.

Next Uni weaves
big leaves
into wings.
"Ready!" Uni calls.

"Flap like this."
Peg moves her wings
up and down.
Her hooves lift
off the ground.

Uni tries to flap.
But the leaves
are not strong
enough.

"I will make
better wings,"
Uni says.

Uni gathers sticks.
Then Uni glues them
with sap.

Uni adds

the woven leaves.

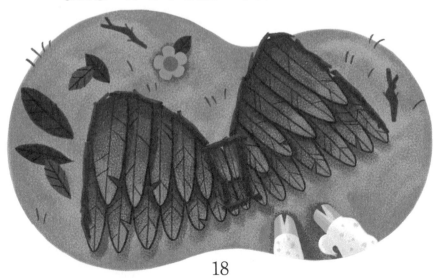

Uni ties a wing
onto each shoulder.

"Run fast," Peg says.
"Then leap
into the air!"

Uni runs

as fast as the wind!

Uni leaps high

into the air!

"FLAP!" Peg yells.

Uni flaps the wings.

The wings lift!
But only for
a few seconds.

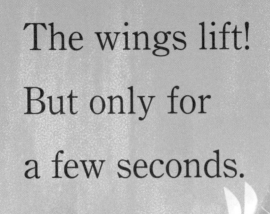

Uni falls,
scaring the bird
in the tree.

The bird falls, too!

Uni's wings
are broken,
but Uni does not care.
The bird
must be helped fast!

Uni's horn glows.

A little cloud forms
under the bird.

The bird lands softly.
Then it flaps
its wings.

It can fly!

Peg soars over
to Uni.

"Are you hurt?"
she asks.
"No," says Uni.

Uni feels sad.
"I cannot fly
like you."

"And I cannot save
birds like you,"
Peg says.

Uni feels better.
"I cannot make wings,
but I can make friends!"

The new friends race
down the steep hill.
The bird soars
overhead.

Peg's wings lift,
but Uni keeps
running.

Uni runs so fast,
it feels just like
flying!